CAME LIBERTY BEYOND OUR HOPE

Came Liberty Beyond Our Hope

A STORY OF HANUKKAH BY LENORE COHEN

WITH ILLUSTRATIONS BY GEORGES GAAL

THE WARD RITCHIE PRESS : LOS ANGELES

8 2 6 4 2.

Acknowledgments to
Jerome Mark Becker and Robert Jose O'Sullivan

⤙⤚

Copyright 1963 by The Ward Ritchie Press
Library of Congress Catalog Card Number 63-18332

for
Ruth and Joyce

INTRODUCTION

HANUKKAH, THE FEAST OF LIGHTS, the midwinter celebration of Jews, is of interest to all peoples, because it celebrates the victory of freedom of conscience over tyranny. If in the year 168 B.C. Antiochus Epiphanes had exterminated the Jewish religion, there might have been neither a Jesus of Nazareth to found the Christian religion at the beginning of our era, nor a Mohammed to found Islam in A.D. 622. It should be remembered that Christianity grew out of Judaism and that Mohammedanism grew from both Judaism and Christianity.

Much of the modern world is indebted to the family of Maccabees who had the courage to fight for the right to worship God in freedom. This concept—the freedom to believe or not to believe, with tolerance for the right of others to believe or not to believe—has become the basis of our democracy. The victory of freedom of conscience is the basis of the Hanukkah celebration.

Hanukkah has much in common with Christmas. Both holidays occur in December. This is the time of the winter solstice, when the days begin to grow longer. Because Christmas is based on the sun calendar it always falls on the same date, but Hanukkah, which is calculated by the moon calendar, varies in its dates from year to year. Both holidays are celebrated with feasts, lighting of candles, gift giving. It is possible both holidays might have borrowed gift giving from Saturnalia, the Roman mid-winter holiday. Northern European customs have enriched Christmas with decorated trees, yule logs, Santa Claus.

Both holidays have become more festive as a result of modern innovations in home decorations, greeting cards, outdoor lighting, parades, and music. These mid-winter holidays have become a time when people think of each other and of peace—sentiments so nobly expressed by the Hebrew prophets. Yet these most beloved holidays might not be in existence today if the Maccabees had not won the right to believe in God, back in the year 165 B.C.

CAME LIBERTY BEYOND OUR HOPE

IN THE YEAR 168 B.C., a little more than a century and a half before the birth of Jesus in Judea, the Jews of Judea were the only people who believed in God. The rest of the world worshipped idols. Antiochus Epiphanes, King of Syria, worshipped the idols of Greece. He was determined to force all his subject countries from Judea to Persia to worship his idols. When the Jews refused to bow down to his idols, he tortured them and killed them. He stole all the treasures from the Holy Temple in Jerusalem, made the sanctuary filthy and dirty, destroyed the Ark, burned the Torah or scrolls of the law, and installed huge statues of Jupiter and Apollo. The Maccabees, a family of Jewish patriots, rose up against the tyrant and defeated him. They cleansed and rededicated the Temple to God, thus saving the belief in God for all peoples in the world. This event is celebrated to this day by the Jewish Festival of Hanukkah, which falls in the month of December.

It all began in Jerusalem on the fifteenth of Kislev, which would correspond approximately to the fifteenth of December on our modern calendar, more than two thousand years ago, in 168 B.C. It was a gloomy Sabbath day; snow had fallen on the land and had whitened the distant mountains in the north.

Earlier someone had started a rumor, *Antiochus Epiphanes, King of Syria, is dead in Egypt!* The rumor spread like wildfire among the Jews and with the snow and rain had come the thunder of revolt. The people rose in wrath against the traitorous High Priest, Menelaus, who had been set in his high place by the tyrannic King. Driven from the Temple in Jerusalem, Menelaus took refuge behind the broad stone walls and battlements of the Citadel of David which towered above the west gate where the Joppa road entered the city.

But the rumor of the King's death was false. Antiochus Epiphanes was sulking within the Citadel, shamed because of his defeat by Roman legions in Egypt.

Now he vented his spleen on the Jews—rejoice over his death, would

[3]

they? The vindictive King with his creature Menelaus planned a fearful punishment for Judea—but he would wait until the Sabbath.

On the Sabbath day the people thronged the courts of the white marble Temple that crowned the east hill of Jerusalem. The Holy Temple, the glory of the city, rose above three terraces, each supported by colonaded archways. Thousands climbed the hill and prostrated themselves before the Lord. In heaven they had none but God, and beside Him they desired none upon earth; to be near God was the highest good.

Nineteen-year-old Simon, the second eldest of his family, prayed near the sanctuary, his cheek pressed against the cold stone. The morning service was about to end, and the congregation listened to the Levites playing their silver trumpets and chanting psalms, just before the High Priest Menelaus pronounced the priestly benediction.

Simon was troubled—so troubled that his heart trembled and tears filled his eyes. He whose heart was filled with the love of God was fearful of the traitor Menelaus. He could not accept the blessing of such a man. Yet he was forced to lie there and pretend to be pious. *I have been pious,* he told himself. *If I had not been a good student of the law, and possessed understanding, the people of Modin would not have sent me to Jerusalem as their representative.* Simon's eyes wandered down the line of twenty-three prostrate men beside him. Some were grey-bearded and old, others ruddy and middle-aged. He was the youngest of the group. Each man had been chosen by his district to go to Jerusalem and observe the daily sacrifice in the Holy Temple and bring back a message of spiritual guidance. Most of the men had been regularly performing this duty every six months. This was the first visit for Simon.

Why can't I be like the rest of them, and think only of God, and not of the wicked Menelaus? he asked himself. *I did think of God and my thoughts were pure when I fasted and prayed from Monday to Thursday. Thursday!* The memory of that day made him bury his head in his arms.

[4]

Thursday was the day when he saw the sanctuary guarded by soldiers! The day Menelaus led the idol worshipper Antiochus Epiphanes into the Holy of Holies, to show him all the treasures, including the treasury of Judea. Then came the sonorous, scornful shout of the King from the Sanctuary, *"This is the living voice of your King whom God made manifest. I now restore as your High Priest and ruler, my servant Menelaus!"*

Now Menelaus, the King's servant, not God's servant, was emerging from the sanctuary to bless the congregation. *He is evil*, thought Simon. *The beautiful robes, the diamonds, the bells, the golden pomegranates, do not make him our High Priest and ruler!* Then the Temple resounded with the sweet high notes of the Levite's trumpets, and the entire congregation joined the singing. Menelaus lifted his hands over all the people, the blessing of the Lord on his lips.

At last it was over. Simon was the first of his group to leave the Temple.

"You look angry, Simon," said an aged man called Joseph as they sat down to the noonday meal.

"I *am* angry." Simon's grey eyes flashed dark. "I cannot bear to be blessed by a traitor who is plotting with the King to harm us."

"Menelaus is our High Priest and you must respect his office," answered Joseph. "God does not listen to the priest alone. Every man high or low may approach God by himself."

"Then why are we sent to Jerusalem to observe the sacrifice?" asked Simon. "I prefer our village synagogues where we devote ourselves to the study of the Holy Scriptures and to prayer without sacrifice."

"The Temple is the symbol of our unity," replied Joseph.

"If Menelaus remains our ruler and High Priest, we won't have much unity," said Simon. "The people should stand up for their rights and drive him out again!"

"Are you telling us to fight the soldiers of the King?" asked another delegate in a shocked tone.

"My father says we should fight for our rights," replied Simon.

Joseph shook his head. "We must meet pride with humility, worldliness with piety. This is the Sabbath, a day of rest and quiet. Let us talk no more of war and unrest."

"How can you ignore war and unrest when it is all about us?" Simon stood up, and from his towering six feet looked down upon his meek and pious companions. "My father says we must always be ready to fight and protect ourselves, even on the Sabbath day."

"I cannot believe that your father Mattathias, who was once a priest in the Temple of Jerusalem, would violate the day of rest by fighting," said Joseph dubiously.

"My father says there is no law in the covenant which prevents a man from defending himself on the Sabbath." Simon shot a defiant glance at the group. "Father left Jerusalem to get away from corruption and passive resistance. Now that he's High Priest and ruler of Modin, the men in our district are armed and ready to fight."

"I understand you and your brothers are the best horsemen and swordsmen in the district," said another delegate.

"Judah Maccabeus is the best," said Simon proudly. "My other brothers, John, Eleazar, and Jonathan, are expert with sword, bow, and spear. But they cannot compare to Judah Maccabeus. He's a born leader. Someday he'll be a general."

"What kind of a warrior are you, Simon?" smiled Joseph.

"I'm as good as John, Eleazar, and Jonathan," said Simon modestly. "I can't beat Judah. He's the best. If he goes after something he gets it."

"Is that why you called him Maccabeus, or Hammerer?" asked the other delegate.

"Yes," said Simon. "Judah is a real Hammerer. But he's very pious and kindly. That's why I say he's born a leader. People love him."

Joseph reminded them it was time to return to the Temple for the afternoon services. As Simon climbed the hill toward the sanctuary, he felt the wind in his thick brown hair and beard. The sky was getting brighter; perhaps the sun would come out. How he yearned for the remaining hours of daylight to pass. At least sundown came early these winter days. Then

he could mount his horse, and go flying down the Joppa road toward home.

Standing on the roof of the highest tower above the battlements of the Citadel of David, King Antiochus Epiphanes waited with his slave Decius, who was also his astrologer, seer, and physician. They were waiting for the sun to come out.

Below in the courtyard was a sea of upturned faces—all eyes on the tall, handsome King in Athenian dress—costly linen tunic, hand tooled sandals, his classic face clean shaven, a laurel wreath in his hair. General Apollonius with his horsemen and footmen, watched the king as if he were a god. The general and his soldiers were waiting for the King to raise his jeweled right hand—the signal to attack the city of Jerusalem!

The King's black eyes glowered impatiently at the pure white marble temple of the Jews. "Look, Decius! The sky brightens! Surely Apollo is driving his sun chariot behind yonder cloud. Isn't that enough sun for me to give the command?"

"No," answered Decius.

"Do you realize we've been standing here most of the day waiting for the sun to come out. Soon the Jewish Sabbath will be over, and if we attack the Jews they will resist us. According to the advice of Menelaus we *must* attack today, because they do not fight on their day of rest." The King chuckled ominously. "We will slaughter them like sheep."

Beneath his high pointed hat Decius' blue eyes regarded the King coldly. He waved his arm so that the stars, sun, and moon on his long flowing gown seemed to move in orbit, and said warningly, "Raise your right hand! Give the signal, and suffer the consequences!"

"What consequences?" asked the King querulously. "Are you prophesying my defeat?"

"I am reminding you that the Romans clouded your conquest in Egypt because you ignored my advice. I told you not to meet with the Roman Popilius on a cloudy day!"

[8]

"The clouds had nothing to do with the loss of Egypt. The Jews betrayed me to the Romans!"

"Your fears, not the Jews, betrayed you," said Decius. "Must I remind you, my Lord King, that you did conquer Egypt, and that you did occupy the country with a large army? Why then, did you allow a Roman to bluff you out of your victory? What right did Popilius have to draw a circle in the sand and say to you, Antiochus Epiphanes, King of Syria, 'Egypt belongs to Rome. *Get out!*' "

"Who asked for your opinion, Slave?" The King's eyes narrowed to slits of fire. "I say the Jews betrayed me! They proved it by trying to revolt when the rumor said I was dead. *I'm alive! Do you hear me, Slave? I'm very much alive!*" Suddenly he let out a wild shout and leaped into the air. "The Gods are with me! Behold, Oh Miserable Slave, the God Apollo drives his sun chariot across the sky!"

"Hold your hand, O King," warned the Seer. "Not until the sun has fully emerged from behind the cloud . . ."

Breathlessly they watched the sun slowly emerge. Yellow winter sunlight illuminated the narrow crooked streets and the square plastered houses of Jerusalem. The marble temple on the hill glistened with dazzling whiteness.

"Now," sadly muttered the Seer.

The jeweled hand thrust upward toward the sun.

Trumpets sounded for battle. The gates of the Citadel swung open. Apollonius and his army charged upon Jerusalem!

In the Temple Simon heard the battle cries. At first he did not really believe they were battle cries. Then he heard clattering and pounding hoofs; horsemen were riding through the temple! Screams echoed around the courts—terrorized screams of women and children! Agonized moans of people slaughtered while praying, "Have mercy upon me, O God, according to Thy loving kindness."

Frozen on his knees, Simon saw the glint of helmets, shields, and flash-

ing swords. Syrian horsemen were riding over prostrate worshippers, cutting down all who tried to rise up! Then Simon was on his feet, and threw his knife directly into the heart of a horseman who intended to mow him down. When the man fell from his horse, Simon retrieved his knife, took the soldier's sword, shield, and helmet, and was about to mount the horse and ride out of the temple when he realized his fellow delegates were still on their knees praying, making no effort to save themselves. "Come with me," he begged the aged Joseph. "It is not against the law of the covenant to defend yourself on the Sabbath!"

"I cannot break in upon the honor I owe the Sabbath," answered Joseph. "Even in such distress our law requires that we rest upon this day."

As the aged man spoke a soldier cut him down with his lance. Simon mounted the horse and fled. He rode to the women's court, and rescued a number of women and children, carrying them out of the temple and going back for more. Suddenly a wall of fire rose up in front of him, for the soldiers had set fire to temple hill. He spurred his horse and rode through the fiery furnace. It was a miracle how he and the horse escaped without a burn; not even his hair was singed. Now his only thought was to reach the Joppa road and make a dash for home.

Suddenly he found himself riding in the midst of the King's horsemen who were fleeing the fire. He could not break away from them, but plunged ahead, and entered the Citadel as part of the troops. While he dismounted, panting and greasy with sweat, a horde of refugees flooded the fortress. They were the non-Jewish residents of Jerusalem and renegade Jews who obeyed the King and bowed down to his idols. Simon seethed with anger when he recognized the evil Menelaus and his followers among the Levite musicians. The traitor was alive and smiling, while the temple courts were strewn with the nameless dead, already forgotten in this dreadful fortress!

"Hey you!" An officer took him for a guard. "Get these people in line, and get them moving toward the sacred grove behind the temple."

"Yes Sir." Simon plunged forward, waving his arms for the refugees to

follow him. Ahead of him was a small but exquisite marble Greek temple, and beyond it a grove of trees. As soon as the crowd began pushing toward the grove, Simon darted into the Temple. Behind a colossal statue of the God Apollo, he found a dark corner. There in the shadow he removed his helmet and shield, hiding them beneath the marble statue. He kept the sword buckled about his waist. Flattened against the wall, he waited for night and a chance to escape, for he dared not stir from his hiding place. At last he was breathing steadily and evenly again. As he watched and waited he became conscious of his torn and filthy robe, and of his hair stiffened and matted with sweat. Out of doors shadows began to lengthen, until the temple stood in pitch black darkness.

Drum, drum, drum . . . pipe, pipe, pipe—high mournful, wailing notes sounded from the grove. Lights flickered through the trees. Slaves came carrying burning torches which they planted around the temple, lighting it up as bright as day. A sacrificial fire crackled on the sacred altar, and tongues of flame from burning oil leaped up and down in two huge urns on either side of the idol. Simon cringed in the merciful shadow that darkened his corner.

Now guards surrounded the Temple, their brass helmets and breastplates gleaming in the torchlight. Black slaves carried the King seated in his golden and mother-of-pearl chair. They set him down on the right side of the Temple facing the idol. The King wore a jeweled crown upon his head and carried a golden scepter; his body was swathed in cloth of gold. Simon found himself looking directly into the smiling dissipated face of the tyrant. It was a glittering surface smile, a false happiness brought on by the wine he sipped continually, for the clay flagon in his right hand was constantly refilled by a slave. To the King's left stood the Seer, magnificent in a long flowing robe embroidered in silver with all the constellations, a jewelled star atop his pointed hat. The triumphant General Apollonius stood at the King's right, and they toasted each other in wine. Evidently this was a victory celebration of the sack of Jerusalem.

Suddenly the drums began to pound, and the pipes became shrill. A group of lovely young girls dressed as Greek nymphs began to dance, and were pursued by youths dressed as fauns with horns in their hair. During the dance performance, an old man in Athenian costume sacrificed a swine to Apollo as a choir chanted, "O Apollo, Father of the Universe, Lord of Creation, accept this sacrifice. Give us light and life!" There slowly entered a procession of men and women, some of them renegade Jews, all in Greek costume with wreaths of ivy in their hair. They brought offerings of fruit, meal, and bird and animal entrails, and placed them at the feet of the idol.

A roll of drums, a blast of trumpets, a moment of silence. The King was trying to rise to his feet, but was too drunk to stand. The Seer and the General half carried him to the altar, where he prostrated himself before the idol. Everyone including the guards fell on their faces. Only the Seer did not prostrate himself.

The sweet acrid scent of incense floated into Simon's corner and sickened him. He had difficulty restraining his desire to leap into the fresh night air, away from the stench of burning swine and the chants of the worshippers, "Great is our God Apollo!"

The Seer helped the King to his feet, held the flagon of wine so that he might drink deeply, then half carried him back to his chair. The people formed a procession, and passed in front of the altar, where they swallowed underdone morsels of swine meat, and were blessed by the ancient Athenian. Gradually the Temple was emptied as people retired to the grove to dance and sing. The King was alone with the Seer and the General.

Now soldiers came forward with chests of treasure, which they opened so that the King might run his hands through the gold coins. When Simon saw the King examining the golden candlestick and holy vessels from the Holy Temple, he knew that Antiochus Epiphanes had robbed Judea of her treasure. The King hit the golden candlestick with his scepter and bent it. "Melt this into coins bearing my name, Antiochus Epiphanes, which will proclaim me as the God made manifest! The god of the Jews is this day defeated! My empire shall henceforth be one people, one religion!"

The King threw back his head and emptied a full flagon of wine, then hurled it against a marble column so that it shattered. He turned to the Seer with scorn in his eyes. "You, Slave, what do your wise eyes see in the stars?"

"There are few stars tonight, my Lord King."

"Which means . . . ?"

"The few will conquer the many."

"*The few will conquer the many?*" screamed the King. "Are you telling me a few Jews will conquer me?"

"If that is your interpretation, my Lord King."

"Swine of a Slave!" The King was livid. "Antiochus Epiphanes will never be conquered by Jews. I will exterminate them from the face of the earth!" He raised up his scepter as a sign he was enacting a law. "I hereby outlaw the Jewish religion. All peoples within the boundaries of my domain shall worship my gods, and eat my sacrifices. Any person who disobeys my command shall die. I further decree that this command shall be written on parchment and delivered to all the towns and cities in my domain. I hereby order overseers to be appointed with the power of life and death to enforce this edict!" The King spat at the Seer. "You, Traitorous Slave, shall die!"

"So be it, my Lord King!" The Seer kneeled down before the King and touched his head to the floor. "How well thou knowest I welcome death and the end of my bondage. We shall meet in Hades, my King. Hast thou forgotten thine own dream, that you were dead before me in the land of the shadows? Because of this dream, thou didst cast me into an arena of lions. While you lived, my King, even the wild beasts refused to take my life. While you live, I live. After you die—I die!"

"Rise up, Vile Slave! Begone from my sight!" The King slumped in his chair and screamed, "Begone—all of you!"

Slowly the Seer rose and backed away from the King. Simon watched with awe. The King was completely in the power of the Seer who was his slave. Here was a man of courage, who spoke what he believed. *The few will conquer the many!* thought Simon. *Is this a prophesy that we Jews will conquer this madman?*

The Seer was now backing toward the pillars where he would turn and leave the temple. Suddenly from behind a pillar a man sprang upon him, upraised hand clutching a dagger. Quick as an arrow Simon leaped from his hiding place and knocked the dagger from the murderer's hand, then stabbed him through the heart.

"Murderer! Assassin!" A guard rushed at Simon and slashed his arm with his sword.

"Here is the assassin!" The Seer pointed to the dead man on the floor.

"Arrest the guards who did not safeguard my life and that of the Seer!" shouted the King.

Soldiers pounced upon the negligent guards near the pillar, and dragged them away to their death.

Simon did not realize that blood was spouting from his arm until the Seer took the cord which girdled his robe and tied it tightly around Simon's arm to stop the bleeding. "I am a physician," he said. "I will take care of you."

"Who is this fellow?" asked the King, so sobered by the shock that he could stand alone.

"I never saw him before," said the Seer. "He looks like a Jew who came in with the refugees who claim to be your friends."

"A Jew in a dirty long robe and with matted beard is no friend of the King," said Antiochus scornfully.

"He saved our lives," the Seer reminded him. "At least give him his life, O Mighty King."

"I give *you* his life, Decius. Take him for your slave." The King drank another flagon of wine and began to laugh. "Slave of a slave! Ha! Ha! Ha! What is lower than a slave of a slave, unless it be a Jew!" And he fell to the floor in an epileptic fit.

Everyone shuddered, even the soldiers. There were murmers, "A demon possesses the King!"

"Leave me alone with the King," commanded the Seer.

Simon saw no more. He had fallen to the floor in a dead faint.

When Simon opened his eyes he was lying on a low cot in a brick-walled room. Cold sunlight from a high window cast a shaft of light on the wall. Zebra stripes streaked the light. *How long have I been lying here?* he wondered. *How many hours? How many days?* He threw back the cover and saw that he was clothed in a short Greek tunic. He felt his face—it was clean shaven! Now he understood the zebra stripes on the wall. The window was barred—he was a prisoner, a slave! There was a mound of bandage on his arm, but it did not hurt. *Thank God I'm alive,* he muttered over and over, until he fell asleep again.

He awakened smelling the delicious odor of frying fish, and he heard the lilt of a girl's laughter. He had vague memories of a girl who had sponged his face and fed him broth. He got out of bed and stood on his feet—very unsteady feet against the cold stone floor. He managed to flatten himself against the wall near the door which opened into the next room, and cautiously peeked in. Crouched on the floor, frying fish at a hearth, was a toothless old woman draped in black. Beside a table stood a young girl shaping cakes with her hands. She seemed like a Greek goddess whom magic had changed into a living girl. Her skin was golden, a glowing golden, against the jet black hair held in place by a crimson band. A long crimson robe draped her slender body, revealing the tiniest of sandaled feet. The small waist was girdled with a cord from which hung fringed tassels. Simon's cheeks flamed and his body glowed as he gazed at her.

The old woman and the girl were chattering in Greek. Simon leaned against the wall for support and listened to them argue about the size of the cakes. "Make small cakes, Diana," said the old woman.

Diana! breathed Simon. *What a lovely name! Diana!* It brought back memories of the happy days in Jerusalem when his father had been a priest in the Temple. That was before Antiochus Epiphanes began his persecutions, when many Jews prided themselves on their Greek learning. Simon and his brothers had studied Greek philosophy, science, and

art. They saw no harm in exercising in the gymnasium which the High Priest Jason had erected under the Citadel of David. His father Mattathias admired Greek culture, but not the vice and wickedness that the King imposed on his subjects as Greek religion. After Menelaus became High Priest by offering Antiochus higher tribute than Jason, Mattathias had moved the family to Modin. In this small town, living among herdsmen and farmers, all the Maccabees became Hasidim, faithful to the Temple and the Law. The slaughter in the Temple had awakened in Simon the desire to return to worldliness. *I am not a saint*, he told himself. *Neither am I so much in love with Greek culture that I would stop being a Jew. I want to study all cultures to make myself a better Jew.*

Now Diana's soft musical voice delighted his ear as she asked, "Ellas, why are you frying all the fish when the King is too ill to eat it?"

"Since the King can't eat it, we might as well have a feast," cackled Ellas. "If he has an appetite for fish, I must prepare the finest and freshest, or he will not eat it."

"Why does the King watch his food so carefully?"

"He ate underdone swine at the sacrifice that opened gladiatorial games in Antioch last year, and was poisoned. Decius warned him that in a hot country it is best to eat the meat of lamb, goat, or ox, rather than swine."

"Now he seems to eat only fresh fish, eggs, nuts, and fruits," said Diana. "If underdone swine poisons him, why does he force the Jews to eat it?"

"Forcing Jews to eat underdone swine is the King's idea of amusement," said Ellas. "He is amused by brutality. Here in Jerusalem he has no arena where he can watch gladiators kill each other or make helpless slaves fight hungry wild animals."

"Is that why he forced that poor widow Hannah to watch her seven sons be tortured, because they would not bow down to his idol or eat the swine?"

Ellas nodded. "It also amused him to have everyone in the Citadel watch those seven young men die. I'm sorry you were forced to join the crowd, Diana. We couldn't leave you alone."

[20]

"It happened last week, and I have nightmares about those boys every night," shuddered Diana. "I'll never forget how those poor boys prayed to God, asking Him to reunite them in heaven. Will God reunite Hannah and her seven sons in heaven, Ellas?"

"Hannah and her seven sons will have eternal life in heaven," said Ellas devoutly.

"Why was the King so cruel to Hannah's seven sons, when he is the father of a son?" asked Diana.

"The King's son is an idiot," snapped Ellas. "He loves brutality because he is jealous of what is good, healthy, and clean."

"Ellas! Ellas! Look out the door at those huge birds of prey still flying around Jerusalem looking for the bodies of the dead!" Diana hid her face in her arms. "I'm afraid, Ellas. Why does this evil King live?"

"God gave him a strong body," answered the voice of Decius the Seer. "The King shall be broken by his own hand. Come, my child! Come, Ellas! Let us kneel down. It is time for our noonday prayers. *Hear O Israel! The Lord our God is one God!*"

When Simon heard these words, he too fell upon his knees and prayed. Thus Decius found him.

"Peace be with you, Simon. Rise up, for now you know I am your brother."

"Peace be with you, Decius." Simon smiled at him, wondering. "How does it happen that the King's astrologer and physician belongs to a people the King detests and persecutes?"

"To the King I am nothing but a Greek slave." He showed Simon the V cut on his ear which branded him as a slave. "I was a prisoner of war, and sold into slavery during the time Antiochus lived in exile in Rome. He saw me caring for sick prisoners, who were to be sold as slaves. Because I am a physician, he paid a high price for me. He suffers from epilepsy and needs constant care. What could be more convenient than to have a physician for a slave?"

"He is also your slave. He fears you," said Simon.

"He fears that his dream will come true, and that he will die before me," said Decius. "After the King dreamed this dream, he pleaded with me to tell him the dream was untrue. When I refused he cast me into the arena to fight the lions."

"You fought lions, and you are alive?"

"God sent his angel Michael to soften the heart of the keeper of the lions, because I had saved his child from death. The keeper fed the lions well that day. I knelt in the arena and prayed, while the lions ignored me."

"What did the King do?"

"He came down to the arena and saw for himself that the lions did not harm me, and he cried, "Decius, Decius! What have you done to the lions that they do not harm you?" and I answered, "God has sent his angel to shut the lions' mouths, and they have not hurt me. God has found me innocent, O King! So before you I am innocent."

"It sounds like a miracle," said Simon. "Your faith in God must be great."

"My faith in God keeps me alive," sighed Decius.

"You must have suffered a great deal," said Simon as he looked at Decius' prematurely white hair, and realized he was still comparatively young. "Yet there is no hate for the King in your voice."

"It is a struggle not to hate the King," admitted the Seer. "Three times a day I kneel, face the holy city and pray to God. His angel Michael guards me from hatred." Then he smiled at Simon. "You must be hungry."

"I'm very hungry," said Simon. "Now I feel very well. How long was I sick?"

"A week," answered Decius as he clapped his hands, and told Diana to bring Simon wash water and a towel.

When Diana kneeled and washed his feet, Simon trembled with joy at her sweetness and beauty. He was glad the shell pink ears did not have the mark of a slave.

After they had feasted on the King's dinner of fish, Decius returned to the King.

Simon was still awake when Decius came into his room late that night.

"You have told me, Simon, that your father was once a priest in the Holy Temple. Tell me, are you familiar with the inner rooms of the Temple?"

"I am familiar with the oil storage rooms, because it was my father's duty to keep the lamps on the golden candlestick filled with oil."

"You do not know of another secret room?"

Simon thought a moment. "Yes, I remember a secret room off the oil room where old scrolls are kept."

"Could you lead me to those rooms?"

"Yes, Decius. Why do you ask?"

The Seer replied sadly, "A most terrible catastrophe will come down upon Judea. The King has ordered the Holy Temple defiled on the twenty-fifth of Kislev."

"The Holy Temple defiled?" Simon turned pale. "Can't we do something? Can't we prevent it?"

"I wish we could; but the King is determined to dedicate the temple to Jupiter."

"Is it not enough he murdered thousands of helpless Jews? Why should he bring his idols, processions, and sacrifices into our Holy Temple?" cried Simon.

"All night the King and the old Athenian have been sitting in the Temple of Apollo drinking wine," said Decius. "The old Athenian has convinced the King the gods will be displeased unless the Holy Temple in Jerusalem is dedicated to Jupiter and swine sacrificed on the holy altar. The King has already sent out a decree that every living soul in Jerusalem and the Citadel shall join in the procession and bow down to Jupiter."

"I won't walk in the procession," said Simon belligerently.

"Hear me out, Simon. There will be much drunkenness and sport. It will be easy to leave the huge crowd and hide in one of the secret inner rooms of the Temple. Now do you understand, Simon? We will escape at dawn, when the guards are sure to be drunk!"

"It will be simple to escape," cried Simon. "I know all the side doors.

We'll have to be well armed—and leave it to me to steal four of the soldiers' horses—but what about Ellas and Diana?"

"It is for Diana I have resolved to escape! Diana is my daughter." He paused. "I have never confided this to another living soul except Ellas. Slaves are not allowed to have families. If we do have children they are taken from us and sold into slavery. Diana's mother belonged to a rich Jewish merchant's family in Rome. We were secretly married, and she died in childbirth. The family thought the child belonged to Ellas her slave. I bought Ellas from the family. It is common in Rome for slaves to own slaves."

"Did Ellas rear Diana?"

"No. Ellas arranged for Diana to be brought up by relatives who live in Jerusalem and are free." Decius strode back and forth. "When I learned of the King's plans to attack Jerusalem, Ellas brought Diana here for safety. You see Ellas is free to come and go at the Citadel. She is the only person the King trusts to buy and prepare his food."

"If I were Ellas I would poison him," said Simon fiercely.

"Then Ellas would poison me," smiled Decius. "I taste all the King's food before he eats it. I even taste his wine. I must live for Diana."

"Diana is the sweetest and most beautiful girl I have ever seen," said Simon fervently. "I will gladly risk my life to help her escape."

The twenty-fifth of Kislev 168 B.C. was a day of deep mourning for all the people of Judea. For Antiochus Epiphanes, it was a day of jubilation. On that day he enthroned himself as a god beside Jupiter, in the Holy Temple of Jerusalem. Swine was sacrificed on the holy altar. While an endless procession of people wearing ivy wreaths ate the underdone swine, the King munched nuts, fruits, cake, and drank wine. All day the Seer Decius stood beside the King and watched the crowd dance, drink, and carouse in the Temple. The old Athenian sat at the feet of the King drinking wine. As night approached the temple courts were littered with sleeping, drunken people. Even the guards were drunk. The old Athenian

was snoring on top of the huge feet of the colossal statue of Jupiter. Wild eyed and hilariously drunk the King flung off his golden robe and stepped into the crowd, bare legged and wearing a simple tunic. For almost half an hour he leapt and jumped with youths and maidens, then fell to the floor in a fit.

Decius faithfully attended the King. He ordered the guard to carry Antiochus Epiphanes back to the Citadel, and made sure the King was comfortable in his bed. Then he quietly stole out of the fortress, and spurred his horse back to the Temple, where Simon awaited him at a side door. With all the guards either asleep or dancing, it was no problem to reach the secret room where Diana and Ellas were waiting. In the dim light of a tiny lamp they knelt together and prayed. "Hear, O Israel. The Lord our God is one God. Blessed be His Holy Name forever and ever."

"I was afraid that a larger lamp might attract attention," explained Simon when he saw Decius examining some of the ancient scrolls in the feeble light. "We have plenty of oil." He pointed to an unopened small cruse of oil standing in a corner.

"Many of the scrolls are at least four hundred years old," said Decius.

"How can you tell?" asked Simon.

"They are written in ancient Hebrew."

"You read ancient Hebrew?" asked Simon in surprise, for at that time the people of Judea spoke Aramaic. "Where did you learn it?"

"In my native city of Alexandria," said Decius as he brought a scroll close to his eyes to examine it. "This scroll concerns a prophet called Daniel who lived at the court of Nebuchadrezzar." He laughed. "My Hebrew name is Daniel."

"You are also a prophet," said Simon.

"I live at the wrong time," smiled Decius. "The scholars of the Great Assembly closed the canon of the Scriptures more than a hundred years ago, believing that all prophets belong to the past. If I were living at the court of Nebuchadrezzar in Babylon, I could be Daniel the prophet!"*

*Daniel the Seer is still alive to us, in the Book of Daniel, the last book to be included in the Holy Scriptures. Many people think the book was written in Babylon four hundred years before, because the real Daniel remained anonymous. It is believed that he really lived at this period of the Maccabees.

Abruptly the drums and the wailing music stopped. Simon crept into the Temple and made sure it was safe to leave. The place was deserted except for a few sleeping guards and celebrants. They hurried past the sanctuary covered with swines' blood, birds' entrails, broken wine casks, and flagons. They ran down a hill to some trees under which Simon had tethered four horses. Diana and Ellas mounted first, and galloped ahead of the men toward the Joppa road.

Just as Simon and Decius were astride their horses and ready to follow, some soldiers came after them. Simon and Decius managed to fight them off, and with the women they plunged through the black night. It began to sleet and an icy wind stung their faces. From the top of a hill they paused a moment for a last glimpse of Jerusalem. Simon said, "Someday we will return to Jerusalem to cleanse and rededicate the Temple."

The storm miraculously cleared as they descended the opposite side of the hill. The stars came out.

Diana looked at Decius lovingly. "*Now*, may I call you Father?"

"Yes, my child."

"Father, can you tell us by the stars when we will return to Jerusalem to clean and rededicate the Holy Temple?"

"I can tell you," answered Decius in a deep voice trembling with emotion. "Suddenly I feel as if I am no longer Decius, the King's slave, but Daniel to whom the Lord has given the gift of prophesy. *We will return to Jerusalem to cleanse and rededicate the Holy Temple in two thousand three hundred days and nights*. Now let us give thanks to God who protects us and guides us to freedom."

Autumn of the year 165 B.C. Two thousand two hundred forty-five days and nights had passed since Daniel, formerly Decius, had predicted the cleansing and rededication of the Holy Temple in Jerusalem. In fifty-five more days it would be the end of two thousand three hundred days and nights, and once more the twenty-fifth of Kislev.

[28]

Simon was now a general, second in command of the Maccabee army of 10,000 men. Judah Maccabeus, the third Maccabee, was commander in chief. The eldest brother John was in charge of supplies; Eleazar, the fourth brother, led the daring scouts who wrecked bridges, destroyed chariots, turned loose horses and donkeys, captured supplies and weapons. Jonathan, the youngest, spied on the enemy.

Dusk was veiling the high mountains painted gold with autumn leaves. Simon and Diana stood hand in hand, watching the dying sun streak the ragged clouds with bands of crimson. Behind them in a mountain cave Ellas prepared the evening meal, and Daniel the Seer bent over his parchment and wrote his prophesies and stories. Many copies of Daniel's stories were passed secretly among the Jews, and did much to rekindle their courage. Daniel predicted victory, and reminded the virtuous and the faithful that even if they endured persecution here on earth, their reward would come at the Last Judgment when the Lord would welcome them into heaven where they would find unending happiness, while their persecutors would be plunged into everlasting hell.

For three years now, the free people of Judea had lived in mountain caves or black skin tents. These mountain encampments were like small towns. Smiths fashioned weapons; women wove cloth and made clothing, cured skins and furs, tilled vegetable gardens. Old men hunted and tended flocks.

Diana, more lovely than ever, was now eighteen years old, and was promised to Simon as his wife.

Simon pressed her hand tenderly. "Diana my beloved, pray for our victory at Beth-zur pass tomorrow. If we rout the enemy, Judah has promised we will march back to Jerusalem. And then . . ."

"Then what, Simon?" There was an expectant tenderness in her eyes.

"You will at last become my wife!" He pressed his lips to her hand.

"I will be the wife of the General of the Maccabees!" she said proudly.

"You will be the wife of the second general," he reminded her. "Judah is our commander in chief."

[29]

"You Maccabees work so harmoniously together," she smiled. "Each brother does his task. No one is jealous of the other."

"We never forget our father's last words," said Simon. "On his deathbed he told us, 'I ask you my sons to agree with one another, and reap the benefits of everyone's abilities. Consider Simon as your father for he is prudent and wise. Take Judah for the general of your army because of his courage and skill as a warrior. Be always righteous and religious."

"I am very proud that I knew your father," said Diana. "He was kind, and had the courage to shelter an escaped slave in his house when we reached Modin."

"My father saw the greatness in Daniel," answered Simon. "My father was the only man in Judea who realized we must fight for freedom. I think of him before every battle, Diana, and of his wonderful courage the day he began this war of independence."

"How well I remember that day," said Diana. "I shiver when I think of that cruel overseer Apelles who tried to force your father to bow down to the idol of Apollo."

"It was the Jew who did bow down to the idol that infuriated father," said Simon.

"Such a low creature," said Diana. "He expected the overseer to make him a friend of the King and give him gifts of gold and silver because he bowed down to an idol. Didn't he realize that Apelles offered gifts to your father because he was priest and ruler of the town?"

"No bribes could induce my father Mattathias to worship an idol. That's why he slew the renegade Jew and Apelles!"

"I'll never forget the surprise of the people when they realized your father had defied the King by killing his overseer. He looked so magnificent when he mounted the overseer's horse and shouted, '*All who believe in God and freedom follow me!*'"

"Yes, Diana, we've come a long way since Father began this war of independence with a handful of farmers and herdsmen from Modin. God grant we will win our liberty!"

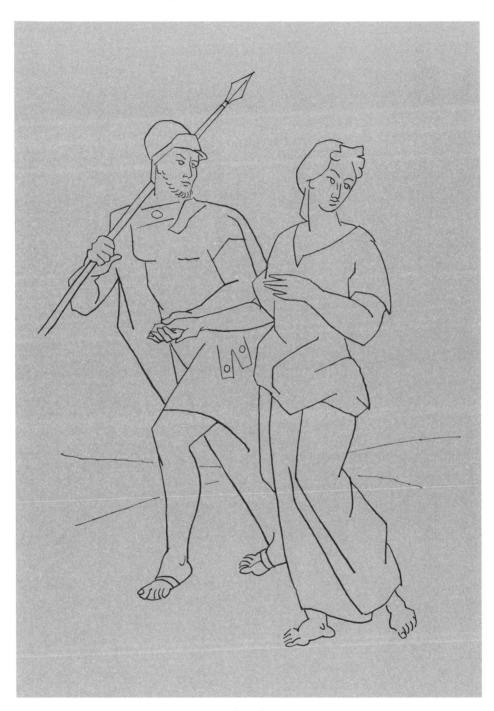

A trumpet sounded for assembly. Out of caves and tents came the troops, hardened mountain men, wearing skin clothing, brass helmets, and shields. They gathered in a meadow, looking up at their commanders, the five Maccabees, who stood on a large flat rock as a platform. The five were tall and well muscled, cut from the same family stamp, with thick reddish brown hair and beards, deep set grey eyes, large acquiline noses, and wide generous mouths. Judah Maccabeus spoke in a deep sonorous voice: "O my fellow soldiers, tomorrow is the time to show your courage and contempt for danger. Almost three years ago my father began this fight for freedom and our right to worship God. Now we are 10,000 strong, united under this beautiful white banner with the blue words, '*Who is like unto Thee among the gods, O Lord!*' If you fight manfully we will gain freedom and the right to worship the living God. Then we will march into Jerusalem and cleanse and rededicate the Temple. Prepare yourselves! Our patron angel Michael watches over us as he rides the clouds on high! Be ready to fight the enemy when day breaks tomorrow!"

"Hallelujah!" The troops sent up a cheer, and marched away singing Daniel's song:

Michael, stand up!
The Great Prince
Which stands for the children of the people.
Thy people shall be delivered,
Michael, the Great Prince,
Stand up! Stand up!

Simon stood beside his brother Judah Maccabeus high on a cliff among the eagles' nests. From this command post, they could look down into the narrow pass of Beth-zur. They could look to the west, and see the plains and the sea; to the east lay the hills of the holy city of Jerusalem.

"Here they come, Judah!"

Simon and Judah watched miles and miles of horsemen and footmen converging toward the pass. Judah said: "Simon, do you realize we are looking at the entire southern army? These are the troops the King maintains to defend the Egyptian border!"

"Now I believe Jonathan's report," said Simon. "Sixty thousand foot soldiers, five thousand horsemen and chariots!"

Judah was trembling with excitement. "Look Simon, how they huddle together under their shields. That's the Roman pattern of a square of shields, and will make a perfect target for our mountain men!"

"Should I give the command to sound for battle?" asked Simon.

"Not yet," said Judah tensely as his eyes followed the column that was now circling the mountain like a serpent. Simon's eyes were on his brother, waiting for the signal. He watched Judah finger the magnificent sword that hung at his side. This was the sword of Appolonius whom Judah slew in battle—the battle in which they captured the huge supplies of weapons, chariots, and food that equipped the Maccabees as a fighting force. Judah's military genius lay in his ability to outwit the enemy, driving them out of towns and villages by surprise night raids. The greatest victory to date had been the defeat of the northern army. Jonathan had reported that the northern generals had divided their army. Judah had tricked half that army into attacking an empty and deserted camp, while he annihilated the other half. Now Judah was raising his hand. "*Sound for battle!*"

"*Sound for battle!*" Simon echoed the command to the trumpeters and drummers.

Beat of drums! Blast of trumpets! Shriek of rams' horns!

An avalanche of boulders and rocks tumbled down the cliffs, crushing the enemy and blocking the road of the narrow canyon. Then the Maccabees loosed a shower of arrows and spears from above. The luckless soldiers of the King fled in fear and panic. Thousands of the enemy were killed. The bulk of the huge army retreated back to the sea, leaving behind horses, chariots, weapons, food supplies, gold, and silver. But the true extent of the victory was not known until a few days later when Jonathan brought the news that Antiochus Epiphanes had withdrawn his army to Antioch. The King himself had gone off to Persia to put down a revolt.

[34]

"Now we have nothing to fear for some time," said Judah. "Let us go up to Jerusalem and cleanse and rededicate the Temple!"

This was the news all Judea longed to hear. The victorious army, followed by throngs of people, marched into Jerusalem.

"War is destruction! Nothing but destruction!" Simon told Diana as they rode side by side up Temple Hill over the blackened brush. Rubble, rubble, rubble—as far as they could see; the standing wall of a house here, a fireplace there.

At the Temple they dismounted and walked through the littered terraces. A patch of glitter reminded them that the columns were bronze under the gnarled vines. The temple yard looked like a jungle, with shrubs grown as high as trees, and nettles and weeds grown up in the cracks of the paving stones. The sanctuary was not only destroyed and stripped of its treasures, but it reeked of camel's dung and rotten unburned sacrifices. Half burned in the ashes were scraps from the holy Torahs.

Then came a roar—a great cheer: "Hail, Maccabees! Hail to our General Judah Maccabeus!"

Simon and Diana went outside and found the hill thronged with people. Judah was speaking:

"We will cleanse and rededicate the Temple together. Everybody, and I mean every man, woman, and child—everybody will help. And everybody will celebrate together when the task is finished."

The people fell on their knees and prayed, "Hear, O Israel, the Lord our God, the Lord is one God. Blessed be His Name for ever and ever."

From the sunrise until the moon hung low in the sky, the people labored to cleanse and restore the temple. Children weeded the garden and helped plant; women scrubbed and polished, wove cloth for new curtains and sewed; men built new furniture, replaced the contaminated altar stones, hammered out new holy vessels and a new golden candlestick. Daniel the Seer helped the scribes write new Torahs. This last was the most important work, for every letter had to be checked by the High Priest.

[35]

Diana and Ellas helped embroider the curtains that covered the Ark. Diana sang as she worked, an impatient little song, because she was so anxious for the work to be completed, for then she and Simon were to be married.

At last the Temple was in readiness. Diana thought her heart would burst with joy when Simon came to see her. But he looked sad and disappointed. "The rededication will have to be postponed, Diana. There is no oil to light the lamps of the golden candlestick."

"Must we postpone our marriage too, Simon?"

"Perhaps for about a week." He took her in his arms and kissed her. "Judah has already sent some scouts for oil. They will have to cross enemy lines, so we have no idea how long it will take for them to return."

"Did they search everywhere, Simon?"

"Everywhere."

"Even the little scroll room where we hid the night we escaped? I remember that there was an extra cruse of oil."

"You are right, Diana! There should be a cruse of oil in the corner of that room!" Simon dashed to the scroll room where he found the small cruse of oil unopened.

"Oil! Oil!" Simon waved the cruse of oil. "Now we can start the celebration!"

"Distribute the oil evenly in all the lamps of the golden candlestick," said the High Priest. "We will start the celebration tomorrow morning, and celebrate as long as the oil lasts."

Daniel's prophesy came true to the day. Exactly two thousand three hundred days and nights, according to the lunar calendar after the temple was defiled, on the twenty-fifth of Kislev of our month of December, the rededication took place, and they called it "Hanukkah."

The winter day was cold, a gusty wind dancing the white banners with the blue lettering, "*Who is like unto Thee among the gods, O Lord!*"

Beat of drums! Blare of trumpets! Shriek of rams' horns!

The procession started at the foot of the hill led by the trumpeters and soldiers carrying the banners. Next came the priests, scribes and Levites in immaculate white robes. Judah Maccabeus rode alone on a white horse, and behind him in a row his four brothers, John, Simon, Eleazar, and Jonathan.

After them the troops, singing:

Michael, stand up!
The Great Prince
Which stands for the children of the people.
God has delivered us,
Freed us from oppression
With liberty beyond our hope.
Michael, stand up!

The people followed the troops waving palm fronds and singing the song of Daniel.

In the temple the lamps of the golden candlestick burned brightly.

Once again Simon fell upon his face before the Lord, and his heart was glad as he listened to the Levites blow their silver trumpets and sweetly chant the psalms:

"I will extol Thee, O Lord
For Thou hast lifted me up,
And hast not made my foes to rejoice over me."

Then came the High Priest out of the sanctuary, wearing the beautiful robes of his office, the diamonds, the bells, the golden pomegranates. Ben Sira, an early sage, wrote:

"How glorious was he when he looked forth from the tent;
At his coming forth out of the Sanctuary!
As the morning star in the midst of a cloud."

The High Priest came down and lifted his hands over all the congregation of Israel and prayed:

"The Lord bless thee and keep thee;
The Lord cause His light to shine down upon thee
And bring thee peace."

Afterwards there was feasting, dancing, singing. Simon and Diana, as they became husband and wife, wondered if a celebration could be happier or merrier. Judah invited every man, woman, and child to feast on the splendid sacrifices and enjoy themselves.

"Diana, I wish this celebration could go on forever," said Simon.

"How long is it supposed to last?" asked Diana.

"Judah told everybody to celebrate as long as the oil burned in the golden candlestick," smiled Simon.

"The lights are still burning," laughed Diana as he whirled her away in a dance.

Everyone danced and sang far into the night, because the lamps were still burning. And the next morning when the priests entered the sanctuary to hold the morning service, the golden candlestick was still ablaze. And it burned, a third day, fourth day, fifth day, sixth day, seventh day, eighth day! On the eighth day the scouts returned with a supply of oil, and the lamps went out.

"This is a miracle!" exclaimed the people.

"It is a miracle of God that lamps should burn for eight days with an oil supply of one day!" agreed Judah Maccabeus. "Therefore I proclaim these eight days, *Hanukkah, the Feast of Lights*. Every year at this time we shall celebrate Hanukkah, and we shall kindle lights to remember this time. We fought for freedom to worship God, and found liberty beyond our hope."

Judea did not win independence until the year 142 B.C. In those twenty-three years, four of the gallant Maccabees were killed in action—John, Judah, Eleazar, and Jonathan. Only Simon survived to become High Priest and ruler of Judea. He erected a magnificent sepulcher at Modin in memory of his father and brothers with seven pyramids and colonnades. The monument was so high it could be seen from the sea.

Simon was greatly beloved by the people, who were free and prosperous during his reign. They began to date their documents from 142 B.C., the year of Simon, High Priest, Captain and Leader. Simon lived very happily with Diana, by whom he had sons and daughters.

As for Antiochus Epiphanes, he met death just as Daniel prophesied, in 164 B.C. while he was in Persia. Rome took over his empire.

HANUKKAH CANDLE LIGHTING CEREMONY

These verses may be used singly each day in addition to the Hebrew prayer as the candles are lighted, or may be used in entirety for Hanukkah celebrations in schools and communities.

First Light:

Each one of us—like me
Is a light.
A Hanukkah light;
First light am I
The Shammus light.
I give flame to all!
Servant light am I.

Second Light:

Each one of us—like me
Is a light.
Second Hanukkah light am I
Who recalls to you Antiochus Epiphanes,
Idol worshipper!
Who tried to stamp out the religion of God.
Defiled the Holy Temple in Jerusalem with idols
    and unclean sacrifices.

Third Light:

Each one of us—like me
Is a light.
The Third Hanukkah light
Tell you of the Maccabees
Who defeated the tyrant
And won freedom for Judea.
Cleansed and rededicated the Holy Temple.
Saved the belief in God for all the peoples of the world.

Fourth Light:

Each one of us—like me
Is a light.
I am the Fourth light who burns so brightly
To always keep alive the memory of Hannah
    and her seven gallant sons.
Who died for their faith,
Rather than live as pagans.

Fifth Light:

Each one of us—like me
Is a light.
I symbolize the cruse of oil
With only fuel for one day
But lasted eight days in the golden candlestick.
Oil, like faith, lasts as long as you believe.

Sixth Light:

Each one of us—like me
Is a light.
Sixth light of Hanukkah, I burn
    to light the State of Israel.
Homeland of the Jew,
Refuge for the homeless and oppressed.
Haven of peace—haven of joy and rest.

Seventh Light:

Each one of us—like me
Is a light.
I am Seventh light of Hanukkah.
I am many lights;
Light of the world,
Light of learning, love and tolerance,
Light to end ignorance and superstition,
Light of usefulness and happiness.

Eighth Light:

Each one of us—like me
Is a light.
Eighth and last light of Hanukkah am I.
Light of a miracle—the miracle of God.
Belief in God lives on despite tyrants and persecutors.
So we pray to God, that He will grant us peace,
That hatred and bloodshed will be no more
That never again will there be war.